I Never Drop Things

An Ivy and Mack story

T0327774

Written by Rebecca Colby
Illustrated by Gustavo Mazali
with Szépvölgyi Eszter

Collins

What's in this story?

Listen and say 🎧 ①

baseball cap

trainers

Download the audio at www.collins.co.uk/839661

shop

shopping centre

Cake shop

"Quick, Mack!" said Ivy. "We're going shopping with Mum. Now!"

Mack put on his coat. He put his toy bus in his pocket.

They walked to the bus stop.

Ivy said, "Let's play the *bus driver game.*"

Mack drew on some paper.

"Two tickets at £1 and one ticket at £2 that's ... £4."

Mack counted the coins.

Mum smiled at him.
"Good counting, Mack!"

On the bus Mack said, "Three tickets to town and back, please."

The bus driver gave Mack three tickets. "There you are."

His name was on his sweater.

"Thank you, Bill," said Mack.

"Can I carry the tickets, Mum?"
asked Mack.

"Yes, OK ... but be careful," said Mum.
"Don't drop them!"

Mack and Ivy played the *bus driver game* again.

"Go left," said Ivy. "Now go straight down the road."

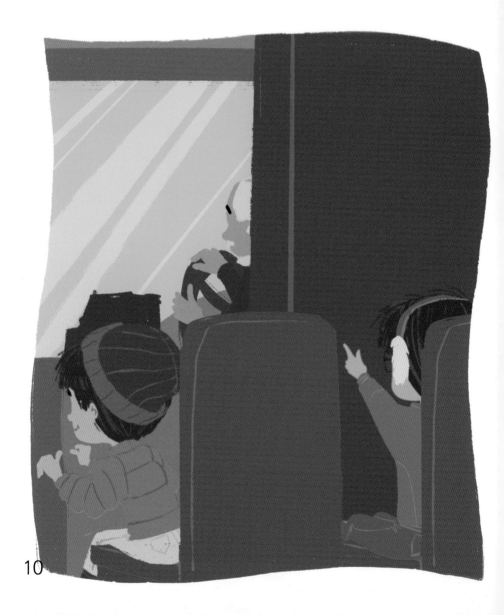

The bus stopped at the shopping centre.
"This is our stop," Ivy and Mack both said.

They went to lots of different shops.
Mum got a new mouse for her computer
and a book for Dad.

Mack got a new baseball cap. Ivy got a new pair of trainers.

And they got a big mango and kiwi cake for tea.

At the bus stop, Mum dropped her handbag. Her house key fell into the road.

"Oh no," said Mum.

Mack pointed. "Mum, the key is down there."

"Can you get a new key?" asked Ivy.

"Yes, but not now. Don't worry. Dad's at home!" said Mum.

"Good! Can we go and eat our cake?" asked Mack.

The bus came down the road.

Mum looked at Mack. "Have you got the tickets?"

"Yes," said Mack. "I *never* drop things."

"No, Mack *never* drops things," said Ivy.

Mack put his hand in his pocket.

"Oh dear! Where are the tickets and my toy bus?" said Mack.

"Oh no! What can we do?" asked Ivy.

"Buy more tickets," said Mum.

"Sorry, Mum," said Mack.

Bill, the bus driver, opened the door.

"Hello! It's you again!" said Bill. "Is this your toy bus?"

"Yes! Thank you!" said Mack.

"I dropped our tickets, too," said Mack.
"Can I look in the bus?" asked Ivy.
She saw some white paper between
the seats. "Look! Here are the tickets!"

When they got home, Mum fixed
the pocket in Mack's jacket. Ivy and Mack
made a thank you card for
Bill the bus driver.

"Now, what about that cake?" said Mum.

"Stop, Mum! Let me get it," said Ivy.
"I *never* drop things!"

Picture dictionary

Listen and repeat

bus driver

bus stop

handbag

key

seat

shopping centre

ticket

1 Look and order the story

2 Listen and say

Collins

Published by Collins
An imprint of HarperCollins*Publishers*
Westerhill Road
Bishopbriggs
Glasgow
G64 2QT

HarperCollins*Publishers*
1st Floor, Watermarque Building
Ringsend Road
Dublin 4
Ireland

William Collins' dream of knowledge for all began with the publication of his first book in 1819.

A self-educated mill worker, he not only enriched millions of lives, but also founded a flourishing publishing house. Today, staying true to this spirit, Collins books are packed with inspiration, innovation and practical expertise. They place you at the centre of a world of possibility and give you exactly what you need to explore it.

© HarperCollins*Publishers* Limited 2020

10 9 8 7 6 5 4 3 2

ISBN 978-0-00-839661-9

Collins® and COBUILD® are registered trademarks of HarperCollins*Publishers* Limited

www.collins.co.uk/elt

British Library Cataloguing in Publication Data

A catalogue record for this publication is available from the British Library.

Author: Rebecca Colby
Lead illustrator: Gustavo Mazali (Beehive)
Copy illustrator: Szépvölgyi Eszter (Beehive)
Series editor: Rebecca Adlard
Publishing manager: Lisa Todd
Product managers: Jennifer Hall and Caroline Green
In-house editor: Alma Puts Keren
Project manager: Emily Hooton
Editor: Deborah Friedland
Proofreaders: Natalie Murray and Michael Lamb
Cover designer: Kevin Robbins
Typesetter: 2Hoots Publishing Services Ltd
Audio produced by id audio, London
Reading guide author: Julie Penn
Production controller: Rachel Weaver
Printed and bound by: GPS Group, Slovenia

MIX
Paper from
responsible sources

FSC
www.fsc.org

FSC™ C007454

This book is produced from independently certified FSC™ paper to ensure responsible forest management.

For more information visit: **www.harpercollins.co.uk/green**

Download the audio for this book and a reading guide for parents and teachers at www.collins.co.uk/839661